WOMAN
OF THE
OLD ROADS

WOMAN

OF THE

OLD ROADS

WRITTEN BY

Juan Rodríguez Pérez

TO JUANA PÉREZ DEL ÁGUILA

CONTENTS

THE TEACHER

HE WANTED to be an agricultural engineer his whole life. First he told his older brother, then his mother, and finally his father. But his father, with austere face and frown, told him that was fine, that he had great aspirations, but that he would have to wait for the farm to produce a little more, "So that, in the meantime, why don't you teach? They need a teacher at Santa Rosa de Mishollo."

"That's far away, Dad."

"It would only be temporary. Meanwhile, you could save money to get to Tingo María and you could apply to school. You'll be an engineer. Besides, son, you just turned eighteen."

This year he made new friends with others who arrived to give classes, and the students treated him like an older brother who guided them. So, even though it hadn't been his intention, at the end of the school year he told his father that he would stay another year to finish saving money for college. But it ended up being three years. When he turned twenty-one, he fell in love with Jenith, a teacher transferred from Sauce who had studied in Tarapoto and was assigned to teach in Santa Rosa de Mishollo. At first he didn't pay much attention to her, but when he saw her smile and shyly pronounce some words, he was dazzled. And from that moment he thought he would stay another year teaching. On weekends he appeared with a horse and invited her to ride around the edge of Don Elías Centeno's land, tasting sugarcane juice or ventisho. He told her about his plans to study in Tingo María to be an engineer and she pretended not to believe him because he always finished his stories by shrugging his shoulders.

His father realized that his son was about to cut short his aspirations, so before he started his fourth year of teaching, he came up with the money and let him know that in a week he had to go to Tingo María to apply to the university and be an engineer, as that was his greatest wish. Douglas, as the kid was called, was sad and made love with Jenith that night. He promised that as soon as he finished his degree, he would return to marry her.

"Do you promise to look for me when you come back?" asked Jenith, rolling around on the straw. "They might send me to another town."

Then Douglas, closing his eyes and kissing her hands, told her with complete certainty:

"I promise."

In Tingo María there wasn't a vacancy. Then a professor told him that while he waited he should study in the same university to be an agricultural technician, until there was a possibility to study to be an engineer like he wanted. For the three years that his studies lasted, he worked hard to gain the esteem of his professors, so that they would recommend him as soon as he graduated. He did the work that they entrusted to him with great effort. If the grass needed to be cut, he did it. If branches needed to be trimmed, he fearlessly climbed the tree. Then he gained the confidence of the rector of the university and the envy of his classmates. Douglas was a worthwhile aspiring agricultural engineer. Every evening, when classes were over, he ran to the river to bathe and then headed towards the classrooms of the university where they were teaching a class that interested him. So they were able to see him in different classrooms, taking notes, asking questions, giving the effort, creating confusion among the professors, who thought that he was just another student from the university. When his academic training was finished, the rector told him that he could continue studying at the university to become an engineer and achieve his dreams. Douglas told him that he wanted to make the most of the break and return to his town to show his father the degree that he had received and to tell him that he was on the way to achieving his goal.

"There will be a vacancy waiting for you," the rector told him, considering the effort that he put forth as a student and his desire to get ahead.

When he arrived in town, he was received with great happiness. They butchered some pigs and invited the town to congratulate the new agricultural technician. He wanted to ask about Jenith, but it wasn't necessary: his closest friends were responsible for informing him that she had returned to Sauce, where they offered her a position as principal. Douglas became sad; but the festivities and the happiness of his family kept him from shedding any tears.

The next day the celebration continued until very late. One of his uncles, the brother of his father, director of a school in the town of Juñao, congratulated him and was grateful that he had returned to practice in the place where he was born.

"In three months I have to return to the university, Uncle," the boy said, squeezing his hand. "No one can stop me from becoming an engineer. I was just waiting for the vacancy that I've earned to open up."

"Congratulations, son! You're the pride and joy of your parents."

Through the entire week, he was smiling at every townsper- [illegible] leaned close and told him quietly:

"Just in case, if you want to work, even for a year, until you save a little money, in my school we need a teacher with your qualifications. The degree of engineer requires a lot of expensive books and instruments that you won't be able to buy if you don't have anything saved up. Besides, you have experience. Think about it, son!"

"Afterwards, nothing will stop me from continuing my studies," Douglas said.

Juñao was far from any river town. One got there by going up and down the mountain that was across from the Huallaga River in front of Huinguillo. He realized that it was a great sacrifice, but it was worth the effort to achieve his objective. These were the stones that blocked him from his goal. That's where he found out that Jenith had married a logger. Then his eyes filled with tears when he remembered his promise and he spent the night drinking cane liquor. He was twenty-five and was the most important teacher in the region. "Don't let me fool you," he told his coworkers, "I won't be with you very long." But he fell in love again, and this time not with just one but with everyone; that made the job easier. So, he was in Zenaida Pichis' arms, he caressed Estefita Tarazona's breasts, kissed Clara Mozombite's lips, and slept in Florida Tuanama's skirts. Douglas was fascinated by the way he was able to captivate the young teachers. Could it be his youth or his aspirations of becoming an engineer? He didn't know the answer. The only thing that he knew was that they loved him. He soon found himself in a mess when he made love to Erma Sifuentes, a girl recently arrived from Lima and furthermore the girlfriend of a young dealer who sold pigs in the slaughterhouses of Juanjui and Bellavista.

The family of the youth swore to get revenge, and his uncle, the director, helped him escape, sending him to a school much farther than his native Tocache, where his aspirations were. There they proposed that he be a professor for training teachers. At first he didn't want to, preferring to return to his town to go back to Tingo María and continue with his plan to be an engineer. But it was enough when they told him that Jenith, the teacher that had made him crazy since he had turned twenty-one and who made love like no one else, was another one of the teachers who gave these lectures, for him to put off his return to the university classrooms. He walked with her through different villages and even though she had a two-year-old daughter who never left her side, he thought up a way to show her his intentions.

"I've never forgotten," he told her when he met her alone.

But Jenith didn't want to know anything about it. She had forgotten now and only wanted to keep a sweet memory. She told him this shortly before resigning from the next cycle.

Before two years had passed, Douglas got mixed up with a student whom he got pregnant, and no one could do anything to save him from the situation. He could only escape as far away as possible, where they would not be able to find him. That's how he ended up working for a lumber company deep in the jungle. He only left at the end of each month. Thanks to his knowledge and abilities, he became a foreman. Before this happened, it had been another three years. He was about to turn thirty, and his aspirations of becoming an engineer were dissipating. His bosses, who were Brazilians and Canadians, valued him greatly, and they [illegible] supervised the making of the main cabins where the bosses and their visiting families stayed. Perhaps because of this, taking advantage of the fact that they held him in such high esteem, he dared ask for a raise for himself and for one of the men under him. The only thing he got was fired. He returned to his beloved Tocache unnoticed.

He didn't want to talk for a long time. Now no one remembered his aspirations. He got into the habit of walking for long stretches and drinking cane liquor at The Junction, Fat María's store, where he met John Clark Shupingahua, Russo Chujutalli, Isidro Tuanama, and Rosendo Apolonio, who talked with him about the boom of the coca leaf business.

"You, you're almost an engineer, you know how to work, you have experience. You've been a teacher and you know how to speak well. Do you want to help us? It's only temporary. Besides, everyone will respect you, no one will mess with you."

Douglas smiled and only then convinced himself that he would never be an engineer.

AUNT LUZMILA

THE WOMAN appeared in the morning, when the sun was getting stronger over us and my father was spreading a sack of coca leaves over the patio to let them dry.

My mother was holding her broom and keeping back the dogs. I saw the woman arrive puffing and panting, dressed in a white dress and a navy blue blouse. She held dark sunglasses in her hands, and a red shawl was protecting her hair. My father raised his eyes and, shielding them with his hands, tried to make out the figure that was getting closer and closer, recognizing her face and her scandalous smile that vibrated among us like an explosion. It was Aunt Luzmila, my mother's sister, the one who left before my grandparents died, trying to get away from this place that had wearied and consumed her.

She hugged my mother with a euphoria that she hadn't even expected herself. She told my father, "How are you, Arturo?" and gave me a kiss on my face. My mother wanted to cry, but she turned her face to one side and lifted her skirt to dry the sweat on her forehead.

She sat on a fallen trunk, crossed her legs, and Dad looked the other way. Aunt Luzmila's legs made him feel ashamed. Mom told her, "Come, come drink something, you must be thirsty." She asked about everyone, Uncle Arnaldo, Margarita, Esteban, and Matías, the little one that my grandparents took care of since his parents had died.

"You won't believe it," said my mother. "He's all grown up."

[illegible]

"No, dear, it's been four years. Remember that my boy is twelve now. Matías is almost his age."

Aunt Luzmila liked to sing. She had said that she would be a famous singer when she got to the city. She used to spend afternoons at the river, modulating her voice, singing to the rocks, to the dry leaves, trying to sound like the birds, singing softly to herself like a Siskin through the roads that took us to the fields. My mother had told us that grandma had had a whip ready for this bad habit of singing when she should have been learning the lessons that she never managed to memorize, and that meant the loss of many years of study. Aunt Luzmila got tired of Grandma's grouchiness and one day just left, not caring that my mother told her that here it was better, that the city was too big for her. Before disappearing, she shouted to us that soon we would be hearing her on the radio, that she would come to tell us everything and that she would take us from this region. We hadn't heard anything from her until now.

"Do you know about Mom and Dad?" said my mom.

"I don't want to talk about it," said Aunt Luzmila, excusing herself. "We'll have time to talk. For now I want to lie down in a cool room."

She had brought a small suitcase with all her things inside. She was dressed like she was going out. We could tell her shoes tortured her. She took them off and, swinging them, came back to hug my mother and went into the guest room.

My father still hadn't said a single word. Despite the

stifling heat, he lit a cigarette and before giving the first puff, chewed the end, spit out a thick loogie and, raising his eyes to the sky, blew out, to spew the smoke out slowly, as if he was reaching glory in it. He saw me sitting at the door, and through his look I was able to understand that my aunt's presence hurt him.

In the afternoon I grabbed my pole, made my little sister come with me, and looked for worms in the hollow, being careful that she didn't slip. I left my mother chatting with Aunt Luzmila while my father was lost in the back of the house. From our position we could hear that the two women were laughing without reserve. My sister smiled, hiding her face when she noticed that this much happiness scared me. We got some worms, and I asked my sister to go back home. Then I got lost at the mouth of the gulley. So I wouldn't feel alone, I entertained myself by singing songs that I'd learned in school.

I came back along the shore of the stream. But before arriving at a well where we would play when we accompanied my mother to wash, I heard someone singing: it was Aunt Luzmila. I crouched down because I didn't want to interrupt her song. She liked shouting it out when she was alone. Hidden among the branches, I could hear her delicate voice and see her naked body, covered with foam. Her fingers ran up and down her back and neck and caressed them like it was the first time. Then she sat and stopped singing to splash water on her face. While she did it, her breasts swung like the oranges of our garden, and a strange shudder ran through my body, forcing me to close my eyes. When I opened them, she had disappeared. I got scared. I didn't move for some minutes. I heard my mom shouting my sister's name. I also heard my father's voice chatting with Matías. But I didn't hear the footsteps of my aunt, who got behind me and affirmed with a serenity that I couldn't understand, "I see that you're growing up quickly. She shook her hair, throwing drops of water on my face.

"Should we go, young man?" she said, offering me her hand "It's getting dark. They'll start calling us soon."

She took off the towel that was wrapped around her and, without worrying about my presence, she slowly dressed, "Sooner or later you'll be seeing these things," she said, smiling with a certain malice.

When Matías said hi to Luzmila, he felt a little shy. He didn't say anything at first. My aunt hugged him and caressed his face, touched his hands, and said that he was a true country boy.

We sat close to the fire in the stove, listening to her adventures, from the first day of her leaving to her return to this town. Then she got up, took a seat on the patio, and watched the stars till my father asked her if she had managed to sing on the radio.

"That isn't important now," she answered without turning her head.

My father didn't ask anything else. He lit his cigarette and went off to smoke close to the garden where the wild cilantro grew.

"Come, Matías, come closer," pleaded Aunt Luzmila. "Tell me how you've been all this time. You must have a girl that would die for you."

Matías looked at me and chewed on some words that I didn't understand. "Come, lay by my side, look at the stars. Do you remember the names of each one of them?"

When I left, Aunt Luzmila was holding Matías' hand.

The next day we got up early. My father and I went to get some clusters of bananas while my mother prepared the coffee. Matías had left at dawn to collect some money for my father. My mother was worried that Aunt Luzmila didn't want to talk about the past. She was always elusive, like she was trying to hide part of her life.

At lunch we talked about a possible party at The Junction on the weekend. She was excited. She told mom that it was a good opportunity to see old friends.

In the afternoon, before fishing, she asked me to accompany her on a walk around the area. She put on a hat, a long, wide skirt with lively colors, sunglasses to protect her eyes form the sun, and sandals. She said hi to Doña Margarita, Aunt Rosa, Don Clodeveo's children, and stopped to hug Doña Martina's youngest daughter. Afterwards we went to the woods to look for worms. She sat on a trunk without worrying that her legs were uncovered. She said I seemed like a great fisherman. I got some worms and went to the shore of the river where my favorite fishing hole was.

"You know that this is my favorite place too?" she said. "I used to come here every time my mother got onto me for singing."

"Did you end up singing, Aunt?"

She looked at me, shook her skirt, and said that it was really hot. Without further ado, she undressed, and I felt that I would get used to her. She immediately jumped in the water, which bugged me because it scared off the fish, and she splashed water on me. Before I could do anything, she pulled me in. She laughed, rocking her naked body when she noticed that I was mad. She hugged me and covered my face with kisses.

"It's nothing, dummy," she said, getting out of the water. "It's really hot and you should wet your head, otherwise you could get a fever."

[illegible] blouse. "I noticed that you like my body."

When we left the woods, we ran into Matías. She asked if he had been watching us. He said that now was when he usually went swimming.

"Wow," she said, "it seems like everyone's favorite place."

Saturday night we went to The Junction. Aunt Luzmila had let down her hair and went with Matías. Mom had her arm around Dad, and I guess I was supposed to do the same with my little sister.

We had a great time. Mom smiled, holding Dad's arm, keeping herself from falling before each onslaught of couples during the pandilla dance. Aunt Luzmila wouldn't let go of Matías for anything. When it was two in the morning, we left. But Matías and my aunt stayed.

The next day they woke up lying over the bags of coca leaves that we had close to the oven. Mom didn't say anything when she saw them eating breakfast.

"There were two men who were watching you," said my dad.

"I didn't notice," she said.

"They were two strangers who arrived a couple of days ago. They're staying in Alejandrina's house."

"I don't know why they were watching me."

"And, you don't know why?"

"Nope." She got up to get a little more coffee. "Maybe they were in love, or they could be buyers."

I couldn't deny it. My aunt had her charm. A little reckless, maybe, but she was pretty. I liked her body, and her breasts that swing like those mombins that fall when they're ripe.

"You still haven't learned to dance," grumbled my dad. "You're the same provocative and reckless girl."

"Does it bother you?" asked my aunt, turning her head and frowning.

My father didn't answer. He looked at her with eyes that said he didn't like her presence and left, slamming the door behind him.

In the afternoon, a little after the sun hid, Matías and my aunt got lost in the woods. Mom didn't say a single word, but dad said he didn't like the way the girl was behaving.

"You never liked my sister," Mom answered him.

"No, because she's always been like that. She falls in love with the first person that crosses her path."

"She's not in love with Matías. He reminds her of her youth."

"Well, I don't like it. This woman is going to bring us problems. I want her to leave next week."

"She'll stay as long as she wants," argued Mom, and upon leaving, she said, "What happened is that she isn't interested in you."

The next day, at lunch, while Aunt Luzmila was visiting the neighbor's garden with Matías, two men on a motorcycle appeared. They wanted to buy the entire harvest that we had dried. They made the deal with my parents and agreed to return on Saturday afternoon. Before leaving they looked around, saying that it was a good farm we had.

A little while back, we had focused on planting coca and selling the harvest to the highest bidder. My parents took the responsibility of drying it in the sun for three hours and then bagging it in jute sacks. We had seen a lot of strangers in the area, some looking for work, others buying, and the rest asking about people who had never passed through these lands.

In the afternoon Dad sent Matías to the town of Cai- accompany him, but Matías said it was better for her to stay because the road was slippery and the horse couldn't take double the weight.

Before three in the afternoon on Saturday, the two strangers who had made the deal with my father arrived and took all the merchandise. My aunt watched them from the kitchen, close to the stove, eating a mombin. One of them looked at my aunt enthusiastically. Smiling, he told his friend that the filly was ready to be mounted.

Mom served dinner before six. She said that she wanted to wash before going to bed. It was really hot. Dad accompanied her to the swimming hole in the creek and sat on the rocks, waiting for mom to finish. He didn't want to get wet, arguing that he had already bathed in the afternoon. When they came back, they went into their room and didn't feel like coming out to socialize. Aunt Luzmila told some stories, but Matías didn't pay much attention.

"Why did you come back?" he suddenly asked while rubbing one of her hands.

"You wouldn't be interested," answered Aunt Luzmila

"Grandma and Grandpa died and you weren't by their side," he rebuked.

"Bah!" she exclaimed. "All the same they had to die, whether I was here or not. You guys go to sleep. I want to be alone!"

We didn't want to upset her. I curled up, imagining her on the mat, placing her butt over the wet earth, putting her two arms under her head, like a pillow, and letting out a sigh as she looked up at the sky. I imagined her afterwards touching her breast, and then getting up to run towards the stream, undressing, and splashing water on her back, her face, and her body covered in tender moles.

I went to sleep with these visions while, far away, a noise bothered me. I didn't give much importance to a shout because I thought it must be part of my dream. But a dry knock at the door and two men that held Aunt Luzmila by the neck startled me. Mom didn't shout. She put her hand over her mouth and looked at Dad with wide eyes. The two men tried to cover Luzmila with a jute sack, but she struggled and from time to time shouted out. Mom tried to leave the room, but Dad wouldn't let her, like he was trying to say "Now isn't the time." Through a crack that gave a view of the scene, I could identify the two men: they were the same ones that had shown up as coca leaf buyers a couple days before. I looked for Matías, but he wasn't in his room. The men dragged Aunt Luzmila to the back of the house. She kept shouting. Once she managed to pronounce my mom's name. The men smiled and said that no one would help her, not even the family, because the jungle has its own rules. Then there was a sepulchral silence. Dad grabbed his breech-loading gun and slipped behind the kitchen. I saw that he was running barefoot. Behind him was my mother. I put on a shirt and tried to look for Matías again. But he wasn't there; surely he had left to go see Zoraida: that was what he usually did when my parents went to sleep early. Since I didn't hear voices, I gained confidence. I tried to make the least noise possible. I oriented myself by the dull moans of my aunt. I stopped close to a clearing, maybe a hundred meters from the house. The man who had said that she was good to be mounted held the jute bag while the other pointed with the pistol. Any minute I would hear the shot that would hurt my heart. One of them said that she had made a bad move, that one [...] an unresolved business, that in spite of having lost the money, they weren't interested in that. After all, money makes itself, but acts like those that she had done, a prostitute of low quality, who dreamed of being a great singer when she only knew how to croon in seedy brothels, one could forgive. They were finishing a mission, and they kept repeating, because they were professionals, and also considerate, because they didn't mess with the family.

"You see Luzmila? After all we're good people. Enjoy your stay in heaven, if they take prostitutes there… Ha, ha, ha…"

A shot was enough to wake me. The door sounded like someone was being careful to be as quiet as possible. I covered my face with the sheet and through a hole could see that Matías had just arrived. I left, looking for Aunt Luzmila's room, and when I was by her side, I gave her a big hug. She gently snuggled with me while saying, "You're sweating, dummy. What happened? Listen, lie here beside me. Did you have a nightmare?"

She covered me with kisses and I slowly fell asleep smelling the aroma of her breath. When I woke, she had gotten up and was packing her things.

"Are you leaving, Aunt?"

"It's time for me to go. I've had enough vacation for a while."

"When will we hear you sing on the radio?"

"Before you know it."

"Will you come back soon?"

"Of course! I want you to show me new places to fish."

She rubbed my hands and pulled my head all the way to her chest. I felt her breathing.

"Come, accompany me to The Junction. I'll find some-one there who will give me a ride to town."

This time my mom began to cry. She didn't ask if she would come back soon or why she was leaving. Dad didn't want to hug her, and neither did she. Matías caught up to us before we got to The Junction.

"Marry Zoraida," pleaded my aunt. "She must be a good girl for you to risk going there at night when your parents are sleeping. When I come back, I want to see you with kids all over the place. Give one of them my name. I'm joking, but it's not a bad idea."

We saw her leave in a pickup. We kept waving for a long time, as if we expected her to come back and stay with us.

That afternoon I went to fish. I entertained myself by pulling leaves off trees and contemplating the fishing hole without really wanting to catch anything.

CARMELITA

THE MAN stopped across from the business going on in The Junction. He threw his bag over a chair and asked for a drink. Carmelita served him, the beautiful girl, María's daughter.

"What does a beautiful girl like you do so far from town?" asked the man, lifting his glass.

"I help my mother," responded Carmelita.

The few who knew him called him "the Colombian" because he had an accent like the people from that country, even though he could have been from anywhere. He didn't try to deny it either. He had arrived with just a backpack and rented a room from Doña Olegaria, an old woman who had lived with her daughters and her grandchildren ever since her husband had fallen off at the edge of the road down a ravine when he was trying to bring three bunches of bananas on his back at once at an age when he should have been taking it easy.

Néstor and I were returning from Don Artemio's farm, who had given us a couple bunches of bananas, and we stopped in at Fat Maria's business. We were hoping she would give us something to drink, even if it was just a little water, since we didn't have a penny left to buy soda. That is when we saw him arrive. He said his name was Jair Casteñeda. He had blue eyes and a ready smile on his lips. I think this delighted Carelita and she sat talking to him the rest of the afternoon. She went with him by our house, heading towards the bank to show him the Huallaga River. On the way back he greeted my mother, who [...] she held the guy's hand and walked with him through the farms. I told Néstor that we should follow without them noticing. With the pretext of going to get guayabas, we disappeared into the woods and we heard him tell her, almost whispering, that he had come to Peru to seek his fortune and had finally found a treasure like her. Carmelita burst out laughing, scaring the birds sheltered in the branches of the trees. When night came Jair asked to spend the night in Carmelita's house because he didn't want to go back to Olegaria's place. María accepted and gave him a place to sleep close to the oven. That night he slept with a machete under his mattress.

The next day, before seven, Mama sent me to buy bread. She told me not to delay. I found Carmelita laying out the tablecloth to serve breakfast, calling Jair, laughing wholeheartedly, which was rare for her, what with her usual constant complaining, when the sound of a horn made us shudder. Three men in a 4x4 truck asked to speak with the Columbian. María got scared and went up to the door to get a better look. She could see that they were the Teacher's men. The boy wasn't worried though; he went out the door without a shirt, slightly sleepy. He spoke with them, and after a minute, they left.

"Don't be scared, kid," he said, slapping me on the shoulder. "They're friends."

Carmelita, a little frightened, asked him the reason for this strange visit, and he said not to worry. María didn't say a word. She served breakfast and I heard him order a rooster to be killed because he was craving soup with a lot of yuca and cilantro. Jair told her he was going to stay and live in their house, and asked them to put him up in a room without fleas or chicken mites. María said yes. And that night she saw her daughter go into Jair's room.

The couple went everywhere they could. At first they walked or rode a horse that they would borrow from their neighbor who lived next to the river. Then, Jair appeared with a motorcycle and no one said anything. Not even Carmelita. She was happy to look good with the Colombian. Sometimes they interrupted us by throwing guayabo fruit at us during the best time for fishing. Other times we came upon them swimming naked and we would hide to watch Carmelita, our eyes growing wide when she kissed him and he squeezed her butt, saying that he was going to make her shout like a mare.

After two weeks we figured out Jair's profession: he was the chemist, the man who gave the "okay" for the cocaine paste. His tongue did all the work. It was enough to just try a pinch of the product that they cooked to know the quality. He became popular among the coca producers. Despite the fact that he said he wasn't exclusive to anyone, the Teacher's men were in the habit of taking him away at any time from any place they wanted, bringing him back the same way. Then we got scared. We, who only sold coca leaves dried in the sun in jute bags to the Teacher's men, knew that his presence would always be dangerous because the soldiers followed his steps.

Carmelita spent all the afternoons she could letting herself be seen in public with Jair. I would look at her, sitting on a stool, how her figure swayed, and nibbling the man's ear. Then she would bring him to the woods where they could shout at the top of their lungs.

The Junction was located in a strategic spot, at the exact dividing line of the roads that led to different towns. And María had her business there selling alcohol, soda, and ... ... could offer, including to the girls who arrived looking for work. So, one could find drug-traffickers, soldiers, police, "partners," and farmers from the area in her store as her customers. Everyone liked Jair, especially the Teacher's men. Nevertheless, Mama told us during breakfast that María had told her she didn't think her daughter's relationship was good. She had found out that her Carmelita was pregnant.

"He's going to leave any day now and you're going to be left with the load," María begged one day.

"Mom, I don't care, he makes me happy," answered Carmelita sharply.

"You aren't afraid of the people who come to look for him?"

"We know all of them. Are you afraid of the 'mule,' Sajamí? You think the pistol that 'Shitari' Pérez carries would fire at you? Mom, please, it's the exact opposite. With Jair here we're protected."

Carmelita was resolved when she answered her mother. She was also resolved when she spoke with her months later, when she gave birth to a baby boy.

One afternoon, when the day was over, some soldiers arrived and took charge in María's store. They asked for soda without putting down their weapons. They joked around, and when they looked at the girls that served them, they whistled to one of them. The one who seemed to be the leader spoke with María. Both smiled, and she offered him a special house smoothie for free. The man looked at Carmelita and shook his head.

"That girl deserves better luck," he said, swatting at a fly.

"One of my men could make her happy."

Then they left without asking about anyone like they did other times. They weren't arrogant and they didn't try to touch the girls that served customers at the store.

Jair, under the pretext of working close to the kitchen that the Teacher was renting, moved away from Carmelita so that he was staying many kilometers up in the mountains, going deep into the jungle, at some farms that she had never been to and that her mother didn't dare check out. The man appeared on the weekends and spent all his time with his son. María would watch him, breathing deep, holding back the urge to grab a machete and follow him. It was Grandma Esmilda who told her one Saturday afternoon:

"That's what men are like! It seems like the more women they knock up, the more powerful and prideful they become."

This kept up until one day when Jair completely disappeared from the scene. No one knew what had happened to him. The Teacher's men searched for him everywhere. They came to María's house and looked in in every corner of their property: in the ravines, in the oven, in the chicken coop. Nothing. The mountain had swallowed him whole. No one knew why. We didn't want to leave the house for almost a week because we were afraid of a reprisal from the Teacher's men. They almost beat Filomón to death just for having mentioned something against Jair. Estanislao didn't have any better luck; they found him floating in the Huallaga River with his throat cut. Weeks later we heard the news that it was the soldiers who had trapped him, thanks to a snitch. Then, just before dawn on Good Friday, close to four, a little pickup appeared driven by a thin man (I know because they woke us up when they parked in front of my house) and unloaded a large sack that was moving and kicking. They went out back, by the garden, where my mother had her mandarins. Afterwards we could hear [illegible] turned off the lights and we hid under the bed. Through the cracks we saw that the woman who was shouting was María, and they were blaming her for Jair's death. Then she, letting loose her tongue, shouted towards our house:

"I know you all can hear me but don't want to do any-thing. Heeeeelp!"

That was the last thing she said. Afterwards there was only the sound of rustling in the undergrowth and knives in the air. The men got back into the pickup driven by the thin man and they left.

The next day, Carmelita grabbed her child and left, on the wide road, without knowing where she was heading.

That afternoon, when it was almost dark, while Néstor and I were resting on a mango tree, we saw a group of men appear who were headed towards our house. We hid, but mama didn't have time.

WOMAN OF THE OLD ROADS

YOU REMEMBER, Ludzina, putting up with the January
rains, in the town of Huinguillo, not knowing if we
should grumble about the rain or about the bellowing of
the cows that were resting in empty houses. And one time
you told me that you had dared defy the Huallaga River by
leaving your goods in Juanjui, coming back pleased with
yourself with some clothes that you always brought from
town. And no one could stop you, not even your grandparents. You learned your lesson, like that time that you saved
me (I don't remember well) from drowning in the "Wild
Bull," those rapids that you had to face many times in a
small raft without many logs. You didn't have time to row
because that was right where "Sepulver" was, cornering
you, wanting to fill you with fear, and you, woman of the
old roads, managed to grab me by the hair and shout out,
giving you the courage to get around the danger.

It's been a long time since my father left home without any
reason. He left with Florida, our dog, leaving a bitter taste
in our mouths, afraid to see us grow, fleeing before dawn as
cowards do, before our grandma woke up and Uncle Jorge
dealt him the blow that he had promised so many times
right after my father kicked my grandma, during one of
his many fights with you.

And you started to take care of the bean garden, shouting in the mornings, scaring off the hens that pecked at

and ruined your plants, and you suffering, shouting shoo, shoo, and us with a stick following, smiling, because it was fun scaring the animals. At the end of the afternoon you [illegible] way, tired from hauling so much water from the Huallaga River, and deep in thought you remembered the time you had decided to escape with Esteban Ríos, far from your mother, thinking that it was the best thing that had ever happened to you. You were no more than a teenager then, filled with dreams about the young man who had recently arrived in town. How were you supposed to know that he would fill you with children that you would have to take care of because he was too much of a coward to stay by your side and watch us grow, take us to school, and help our grandma with the desks and chairs that each student brought at the start of the school year.

You used to chat with Eliobina, Ruperto, Blanca Sánchez, and others who stopped to check out the chicken coop that you had at the entrance to our land, so that they would be envious of the amount of hens we raised, so many that we didn't know what to do with all the eggs and chickens. Then you would load your raft without caring that the river was up and the rapids could take away your goods, even your life, and you would go to Juanjui to barter. You used to come back on foot, walking the 27 kilometers between the two towns, crossing the river, sometimes swimming, protecting your new clothes by holding them above the water with a forked branch you held above your head. When you got back home, you were happy, saying that you were proud of having let your husband leave, even though we knew that, in your heart, we needed an extra hand to help us in the garden and to take care of the animals. That is why Grandma sometimes helped, keeping herself busy fixing the enclosure or putting a roof on the chicken coop.

Then, enjoying a cup of coffee, sitting on a mat of uricuri leaves, you told us the story of your life once again, from the moment that your father fell in love with Juana. And Juana, playing hard to get, made Florentina, her mom, angry. Not listening to anyone, he went with her into the woods for an evening show where Juana was presenting, and escaping during the intermission, made the most of the situation. You liked to remember this, and we had heard the story so many times that now we had it memorized. Your father fed them fish every day and also shared it with the people of the town because he was generous. He sent you to his mother, Grandma Santo, to give her a serving of black prochilodus, even though she would then order you to toss it into the pigpen without explanation, because she never accepted Juana as her daughter-in-law. And you laughed, hiding your face full of moles. Finally, you remembered the time that you gave a katana to your friend from school, one rainy afternoon, and you fought hard for almost an hour and only stopped because it began to get dark and your friend couldn't take the volley of blows that you dealt her any more. Though you had been furious at the time, when you finished the story, you got sad because you couldn't remember the reason you had been fighting.

When you met Aquiles Rengifa, the years had already begun to catch up with you and happiness was fading, making you nostalgic. And with him we went to live in Tocache, far away, as if we were trying to forget all those memories of my father. The river, the raft, the machete, the mare, the three dogs that they gave us when we came to live in this town, and as many animals as we were able to raise were our companions in our excursions through the woods. That was where we saw you digging in the humid earth, planting and caring for the coca plants so that they [illegible] for sowing, because there was someone called the Teacher who paid a good price, and a Colombian who offered his services to the highest bidder to give the "okay" to the coca production. And you cried one afternoon when it suddenly poured down rain because you didn't have time to bring in the leaves that were drying. But happiness came back to you, even though your body was starting to hurt in old age. People would look at you with pity because your legs had swelled up and it made you limp when you walked. Nevertheless, you had the prettiest farm; you began to take care of the animals that got lost in the woods again. You were happy, even though we never liked the business you started selling beer, because that's where the thing began. You were Fat María's competition; she had her store at The Junction. And her enemies ended up being your enemies.

When I think about you, I feel proud to be your son, and ashamed for not knowing how to defend you when they came to take you from the house, saying you were to blame for Fat María's death, an accomplice for not having defended her in spite of the woman's shouts. You saw the light of day cut into a thousand pieces in the back of our land, close to the chicken coop, before dawn on Holy Friday. They took advantage of Aquiles Rengifo's absence to condemn you and make of you what life couldn't.

Luzdina, now you are resting after a long journey, and your eyes sleep like butterflies resting on a flower.

HORTENSIA

A UNIFORMED YOUNG man stood in front of her, firm, with his hand on the trigger and the face of someone without many friends. Some words flew out of his mouth that Hortensia understood all too well.

"Partner, will you at least let me feed the animals?" the woman asked, getting up. She put the bananas that she was peeling for lunch to one side and set out to look for corn. "I hope their water lasts till we get back."

The man didn't say anything. He knew Hortensia, the old woman who worked these lands together with her husband, Misael, and her son Antonia, and he signaled for her to hurry. The woman walked slowly. She was alone because the men of the house had to go to Campanilla. Partners, as the townspeople called the young men who became involved in the internal conflict, were in the habit of appearing in one of two ways: one, they came smiling, greeting you politely, raising a hand and saying that there was a meeting at so-and-so's house; and the other was when they appeared in uniform, with hardened face, their hand on their belt or on their weapon and making signs for you to follow them. The latter was a bad sign because it was an order that one couldn't escape and had to just obey. The bad part about these meetings lately was that they could last two or three days. That was why Hortensia was worried.

She brought a plate, a cup, and a spoon. She closed the house and the small store that she had, even though it was just a formality, because if someone wanted to come [in the night ...] the door.

"Will it take long?" she asked for the sake of asking.

The man didn't respond.

"I'm alone, my husband and children still haven't come back, and my animals are going to die of hunger and thirst if we take too long," she insisted, but it was in vain. The inscrutability of the man left her without the desire to ask any more questions.

She had already lived through one of these experiences. It happened when they had tried Leocadio Fasabi, and all because of a woman who had accused him of stealing a pair of hens. No one spoke up for him, only old Ruperto, who dared to timidly question the partners' attitude. One of them, the one who seemed to be their leader, asked if his experience as a union member in a ceramic factory could be of use to help him in this situation. He replied that a pair of hens didn't have the same worth as the life of a man, and if they wanted to show that they were capable of judging a person with greater equality, then they would win his admiration. Everyone remained silent. Old Ruperto lowered his head and closed his eyes when the leader of the group got close. "What do you think we should do then?" he asked, pulling Leocadio. "It isn't the first time."

"Then cut his neck," said Ruperto, settling it, at the same time that Leocadio's wife let out a shout that made the forest shudder. He had said it without raising his head.

Everyone was gathered in the forest where they had been led, far from town, walking almost the entire day, until they arrived by a river in a ravine where a group poked at bananas and some game on coals. On the second day the leader decided it was time to judge the people in accordance with the reports that came to them from the partners who carried out this mission. Suddenly Hortensia remembered the visit from the two boys looking for work. She remembered them well. They had slept in her house, on the roof, close to the sacks of coca leaves that had been dried in the sun. The next day, early, the boys had walked through their land, asking the workers questions and smiling, asking for more food, and she serving, without denying them anything. She remembered too that she had had some arguments with some of the townspeople because of the credit that she didn't give in her store. She didn't want to remember any more. The image of Leocadio stayed in her mind, sitting on a trunk next to a "partner" that watched him, while the leader continued speaking with Ruperto.

At the crossroads that led them to Bajo Limón, they met with a group of townspeople and headed towards the forest. No one said a word. Fear could be seen in the faces of each one of them. From time to time the shrill voice of the partners could be heard giving orders when one of the townspeople murmured more than they should have. She didn't know the road because they were in the habit of changing the route to avoid a possible snitch that would give away their location. At times she slipped because of her age. Her sixty-eight years kept her from following the same rhythm as the rest. There was always someone behind the column, urging them on. Suddenly she tripped on a root and fell over a mound of dry leaves. She didn't want them to help her get up. She brushed off the wide pants that she wore, adjusted her rubber boots, and kept walking.

After two hours of hard traveling they stopped in a clearing in the forest. They ordered a fire be made to cook a light meal. They boiled bananas and put dried fish on the [illegible] some water and put out the fire. With green branches they swept the place, scattering the ashes in the forest. The one who seemed to be the leader lit a cigarette and breathed deeply, sending puffs of smoke into the sky. He didn't look at anyone. They finished setting up camp that evening.

Hortensia estimated that they would stay for a couple days, so she settled herself under a capirona tree and decided to close her eyes for a minute. It was then that she remembered the threats that Rómulo Fasabi had made about her bad treatment of the laborers. She was usually strict when there was work to do. She only asked for what they charged per day. If Rómulo felt offended it was because she didn't want to credit him beer. And he had threatened her. Shortly after that these two boys had appeared, skinny, with smiles on their faces, asking for some food and begging her to hire them as laborers in the coca leaf harvest. She was doubtful at first. Who could hire just anyone? Besides, she had a lot of workers already and the harvest was small. But all the same she took them in, and after a week Rómulo came back asking for beer, saying he'd pay her back as soon as he harvested his product, and she denied him. She grabbed a stick and followed him, called her dogs and then, Tilico bit him. She said, "You deserve it. And go before I call Ringo. He won't leave you with your health."

Suddenly she felt fear because her husband wasn't close. The boys she had taken on as laborers were talking with their leader. It had been about a month since Fat María had been murdered and no one had had the strength to defend her when they had her in the foliage, behind Luzdina's house, when she had been shouting. They had just turned off the light and afterwards Luzdina heard a lot of shouts. The next morning, almost in a whisper, they said how Fat María had been killed by men that she didn't know. On the afternoon of that same day, they killed Luzdina. No one knew if it was the same men. They dragged her like a pig and brought her behind the house, and her shouts were lost among the forest and the coca leaves. That was when Hortensia decided to bring her report to the police station. But they didn't take her seriously.

Night came fast and they remained in darkness because the leader didn't let them light a fire. Hortensia wanted it to rain so that she wouldn't feel the mosquito bites or the oppressive heat. She felt that her blood pressure was rising. She wanted to get up and walk to the river, but she stayed immobile, trying to identify the sounds that were mixing together in the undergrowth.

The next day, before six, they were woken and served a little tuna with inguiri left over from the day before. The leader called them and ordered them to get in line. The women were to line up in back, but let their faces be seen. Each person was mentioned. She remembered Leocadio Fasabi, the time that they accused him and thanks to the intervention of Ruperto, he only got thirty lashes in front of his woman. She smiled because she would have had the same luck if they hadn't listened to Rómulo. Maybe her strong personality had betrayed her, but they weren't bad people. The young men who went to her farm asking for work could testify to that.

The ringleader started a discussion that she couldn't understand. He lowered his head and one of the young men raised his chin. The man continued speaking and she still didn't understand until she heard her name mentioned and then she felt needles in her spine. She didn't [illegible] that hung over the leader's head. As if floating away, scenes came to her of when they took the two boys away in a helicopter, when the streams filled with dead fish, when the light of dawn exposed floating bodies in the river, or of a shout that she heard one time in the middle of the night without knowing where it came from.

That was when she heard the sound of death, a sound that ripped through one's clothes and destroyed the silence. A horrifying gust went over the plants and the many people in its path. A helicopter had discovered them and began to fire without asking for forgiveness. They weren't asking nor dared to answer questions. They only acted.

Hortensia threw herself down and saw the leader lying on a bed of dry leaves with his cranium destroyed. She ran for her life. The bullets followed and she heard shouts behind her back that hurt her more than they should have. She remembered that she was sixty-eight years old, but even so she still got around liana, roots, and even thorn bushes. She didn't know how long she ran, nor did she remember when she had left behind all the people who shouted crazily, being punished from a helicopter without pity. She found refuge in a small cave that she came across on the shore of a creek.

She got home before five in the evening and felt sad, without hearing the noise that her animals usually made. One of her dogs came close and began to lick her feet. Out back were the chickens, having died from hunger and thirst. Some had begun to be eaten by the dogs and other animals.

At six her husband Misael and her son Antonio arrived and they found her sitting, close to the oven, caressing one of her dogs, moving her head, letting out bitter tears, without daring to respond to the touches of her husband.

She knows that they will come back any time, but she doesn't know who they'll be or when they'll come…

THE FIRST TO RAISE THEIR HAND

WE SAW him disembark at the port at the beginning of February, before the carnivals started, when people came out of their houses to throw water and flour on whoever crossed their path. Then a hot day finally arrived and the village got a rest from the seasonal rains.

It was midday, and the sun hurt his hazel eyes, fair like the hairs on corn. Straight ahead there was an enormous plain where one could make out animals that looked like far away dots. He shielded his eyes from the sun with his hands and tried to make out the few townspeople who were buying and selling at the port. One of them came up to him and, extending her hand, greeted him. A girl was swinging happily in a hammock slung to the trunk of a lime tree. We laughed as we watched him struggle with his load, and when we went up to him to offer to help, we noticed how tired he looked from the long journey. He looked at us with pleasure and let us guide him to Doña Margarita's lodgings, where we left him cooling off with a lime aid that she knew to offer the recently arrived.

In the afternoon we saw him standing at the doorway of his lodgings. He stretched his arms and surveyed the street with a glance. My little sister laughed, because she is like my mom who laughs at everything, bugging my grandma. Since we only lived four houses down the street from Doña Margarita, it was easy to watch him. It wasn't that he was weird or anything, just that he was new to town and the newly arrived are the talk of the week. We found out that he was a teacher and that he came to replace Doña Nativi-

one dared to work in a remote village with a single street, where so many children wandered around like animals. Mama didn't ask about him, like she usually did when a stranger appeared, but simply restrained herself to smile when she learned about his arrival. She told us he had mentioned in the port that his name was Reyder, like my father's.

We saw him go out religiously to the river, every morning before seven, carrying his towel and soap for washing his face and mouth. Afterwards, he would remain sitting on a rock, watching the girls that came to get water. In the afternoons he sat in a rocking chair, watching the rain fall, sleeping with the dense fog that formed in front of him. We wondered how long he would stay, and we bet that next year we'd have a new teacher. When the weather cleared up, we had fun watching him swipe at the air trying to scare away the mosquitoes that were imbedded in his young and unexplored body. At the end of February his leg had swelled up, despite the fact that he went around covered in thick sheets, in a vain attempt to protect himself from the mosquitoes.

At the beginning of March he took part in the village's activities, especially in roofing the school or making repairs. Each one of us had a job: getting a palm leaf, tamshi vine, reed or balsa wood, making clay to cover the walls, weaving the urucuri leaves, or fixing the fence. Some of the women simply made orange juice or limeade with cane molasses, or provided fruit for the workers. Some got into groups or found a partner, so that there would be a sense of organization when decisions had to be made. On one of these outings Mama and the teacher worked together. When the day was over, she came home content, spoke more than usual during dinner, and didn't stop even when we took out the mats after dark to contemplate the sky and be filled with Aunt María's and Uncle Atilio's stories. She said that she was fond of the teacher, even though his long hair bothered her and his crooked teeth made his smile ugly. She thought that he was polite, and he almost didn't let her do any of the work that was planned. Mama had always been cheerful. Still, we had been surrounded in sadness since Papa passed away, so we were happy to see her enthusiastic.

When we got to know the teacher, we began to love him, because we could observe him closer during his frequent visits to our house. To tell the truth, he had a sincere smile. His eyes were small, but they set on you attentively in a way that couldn't be evaded. He had conviction in his decisions. When class was over, especially on Thursdays, we spent time together in our weekly walks. He told us about everything he had learned in the big city. He didn't like people who were lazy, and repeated it every chance he could. Every night, at eight, he went around town with a lantern, and greeted every one of his students, briefly, making a comment about what we'd been reading or giving us instructions for the homework. On Saturday afternoons he would visit our house and remain seated on the pavement outside, listening to the stories that Uncle Atilio told about his many trips to the mountain to hunt wild animals. The stories fascinated him and once he even mentioned that maybe they could be published one day. Mama stayed with him and we watched from a crack, let him say goodbye without bothering them, thinking we liked how the teacher kept Mama company. At the end of the year we decided to live [illegible]

Once he told us that he would take us to see Lima. But he was never able to carry out his promise.

Around this time the villagers began to plant coca leaves because people came from far off places and offered a good price. No one raised animals nor grew anything that wasn't coca any more. Other products became scarce, but this wasn't important because people could afford to pay the asking price of the goods they needed. The corner stores that before had stayed mostly empty, with a regular customer from time to time, were now packed. Loud music poured into the streets and women began to arrive who upset the village. It turned into a no man's land. The teacher didn't go out at night any more to visit his students because he was afraid of getting hurt. On more than one opportunity, they ended up making fun of him and threatened to throw him into the river.

Sometimes a police patrol arrived and set up in the surrounding area. They checked every villager who crossed their path, patted down their hands and feet, the sacks they carried, and even insulted them. One afternoon the partners appeared heavily armed and then the villagers really did begin to live a nightmare. Shots were heard late at night. We tried to figure out if it might be the police standing up to the partners or the dealers. We didn't know, we could only guess. The next day rumors ran wild. Sometimes the village got a break from this activity for months, because the coca leaf buyers entrusted the young men from our area to harvest the plants, hire a kitchen, process it, and bring it to the boss. In the areas surrounding the village, bars appeared, attended by underage girls who wished to please their customers. Once Reyder tried to call attention to this wrong, but he was threatened. And he withdrew, feeling that this humiliation was going to hurt him for a long time.

One morning, when the roosters hadn't finished crowing for the first rays of the day, the partners appeared completely armed, shouting to the young men of the village to unite for their cause. Many were frightened at first, but then when they saw them speaking with the teacher in the school, they came up and were convinced to enlist. At first, it was the boys who showed enthusiasm, then the girls, until it became common to see them leave for three months, then to come back in uniform, shouting like animals, driving fear into the villagers. The partners gave responsibilities to the young men who showed inclination to keep the village pacified.

The village was filled with a false happiness that would hurt Reyder for a long time. The people crowded into a corner of the highway, at the exit to the town, more or less a half-kilometer away, called The Junction. A lot of beer was sold there, and the girls offered themselves to the highest bidder. They came from all corners of the country, until a Colombian arrived for whom the men were waiting in line until past three in the morning. Sometimes shots rang out.

On Friday afternoon three helicopters appeared packed with police. They didn't ask questions. They took possession of The Junction and arrested all the villagers that were there. Then, they headed towards the school and took the teacher. My mother followed them, shouting not to take him, asking what was his crime, but they, without paying attention to anyone, left. They took maybe twenty more young men. We never heard anything from them again. Mama, that night, took refuge in the backyard and cried

come back some night all muddy and tired. The mothers of the rest of the young men got tired of asking around in all the jails.

Months later, when the partners arrived in the village in uniform, with their arms on their shoulders, shouting, and asking who wanted to enlist, Mama was the first to raise her hand.

MAGNOLIA

MY FATHER pointed out the figure of a man who got off a motorcycle. He told me that he was the Teacher. He said it timidly, as if he was afraid. I had just arrived from Lima and weariness was pressing down on my shoulders, so I didn't pay much attention to this figure who I would later recognize as someone to be careful around.

We set off down the road and headed toward the farm that my parents had bought. It was out of the way, maybe ten kilometers from town. There my mother had dedicated her time to growing coca.

It was common now for all the farmers to harvest coca leaves. We took advantage of every possible space on our land for this activity because there was someone who paid a good price, and in advance: the Teacher.

My mother crossed herself when she saw me appear. I was sweaty, very thirsty, and worn out from the heat. She said that she didn't think I was coming, knowing that I was a police officer on vacation.

"I asked them, son," said my father, "if you could spend your vacation here. They said that if you didn't mess with them, they didn't have a reason to mess with you."

I was a little scared. The area was very dangerous, a completely red zone that was dangerous for any police officer. But the urgency to see my parents, who didn't want to return to Lima, helped me make the decision to visit them, in spite of the risk.

"Don't worry," I said, hugging my mother. "I'll only be

In the afternoon my father showed me the river. Then, we went to see a stream that ran behind his field. Dead fish were floating in it; it seemed strange.

"Someone is 'cooking' upriver, above the ravine," said my father. "That's why the fish die. All the acid and the mixture that they use to process the coca leaves go into the stream, poisons it, and kills the fish. Downstream, almost at the river, the people collect and eat them."

Suddenly we saw two men coming up to us. One of them had a machete in his hand, and made as if he was cutting some plants.

"Passing through?" asked my father.

"Don Eshtaquito," said one of them, "we're processing. We thought that you were snitches, but I guess not. This man is your son? Nice to meet you."

I tried to smile when he extended his hand. The other man didn't come up to us. He stood close to a banana tree trunk. He talked with my father and then, before saying bye, asked me:

"Do you play soccer? Tomorrow we'll be on the field, see if you feel like it. And afterwards, I'm sure you know, we'll drink a couple boxes of beer. Don't worry, it's on me."

I looked at my father and he, becoming serious, pointed out:

"My son will only be here a couple days."

"Don't worry. What's your name, man?"

"Artemio," I said, and I looked him in the eyes.

"Well, Artemio, tomorrow afternoon we'll see you on

the field. Your dad already knows where."

We watched them walk off. My father said that they already knew I was a police officer. I felt a little scared. I knew that if I took one wrong step, they would be pitiless. Maybe they were scaring me for fun. My father took a bunch of bananas and tried to carry them. I beat him to it and he said that my shirt was going to get stained. "Besides, you're from the city," he remarked, laughing. I didn't listen to him.

When we got home my mother had slaughtered a chicken and cooked it in the local style: on a skewer over coals.

"You can smell the canga from far off and it wouldn't be strange for some guests to appear."

She hadn't finished speaking when we saw a girl come up who was walking slow, tired, and carrying a cloth bag in her hands.

"It's the crazy Magnolia," said my mother. "Every once in a while she appears around here, when her boss lets her go."

I didn't remember the girl. But when I saw her up close and she stamped a kiss on my face, I remembered that a young girl had been living in my house a long time ago and that she disappeared after turning fifteen. But that girl had been really skinny, and hadn't wanted to eat. I didn't know for sure why she had disappeared, even though a few tasteless people had said that it was because they had found her in bed with my cousin César and they hospitalized her when she got pregnant; and from there she had escaped. That was a long time ago. But this Magnolia was very much a woman. Her eyes laughed and everything about her was a party.

"Aunt," shouted the condemned one, "it seems like I came at a good time."

"Don't you remember her, boy?" asked my mother. "Come! Sit, we're having a barbecue. Old man, serve the mingado."

I tried to remember her, but the images got lost in my [illegible] though I tried, I couldn't take my eyes off her. My father noticed and remarked within hearing,

"Magnolia is a whore."

After eating I lit a fire behind the house and kept looking at how the coal sparked and mixed with the lights of the fireflies. My mother said that she felt like sleeping early because she was very tired and tomorrow, Saturday, she had to dry some leaves before noon. My father laughed with Magnolia. She was sitting with her legs open and chewed on strands of her hair. Soon my father went to bed. I said that I'd stay up a little longer. And she spoke to me,

"You have courage coming here. The Teacher knows that you're a police officer?"

"I don't know who the Teacher is, and I don't really care."

She was quiet for a minute. Then, as if she didn't care how I answered, she asked:

"Do you know what I do?"

"Why would I need to know?"

"I'm his favorite whore. Don't ask me how I ended up that way. When they told me that Don Eshtaco's son had arrived, I said shit, what's that guy doing here? The men you met in the field told me. The Teacher already knows that there is a stranger in these lands. He'll be watching you."

"I'll only be here a week."

"Tomorrow you have to go play. They invited you and you have to participate. I'll be there. Now, tell me, what news from Lima?"

I smiled. The condemned one realized she had scared me. She kept talking because she felt like it. She was missing a tooth and from time to time she covered her mouth because of it. "I didn't want to be a whore," she said, and began to tell me that she had arrived, together with her friend, from Pucallpa, looking for work. She ended up working in the bars, serving the regulars. The boss had told them that they had to satisfy the customers if they didn't want to look for another bar… And that's how she ended up lying with whatever drunk wanted it. "Until one night, around nine, a man arrived who was dressed well, accompanied by two young men who were stationed close to him, and they called me over. The Teacher, as they had begun to call him then, asked my name and how old I was. Then he invited me to sit next to him and ordered a box of beer. He opened two bottles and the rest he handed out to the regulars that were in the bar. 'Do you want to work for me?' he asked, pronouncing the words almost like music. 'I'll dress you well and you won't have to come to this bar any more. Tomorrow we'll go shopping. And afterwards we'll go on a drive to the town of Sión.' I told him that I was with my friend Leonor and he said no problem. Leonor didn't want to go with me, but in the end I convinced Leydith, a girl from Moyobamba that had just arrived in Tocache. The next day, with our new shoes and clothes, we went on a trip. That night we slept with him, but the night after he rented us out to his friends and any dumbass he wanted. At first I cried, and refused. Then, I got a beating that almost left me unconscious. I had to hold back my tears because I had no other choice. After two days he came back to us and said that he would visit us once a week. Before leaving he gave us more cash than we could have imagined, because for us, it was more than a week's worth of work."

"I hope you win," she said, and she left.

✳ ✳ ✳

"You're here," the man I met in my father's field told me. "I'm Isidro Tanama. Let me introduce you to the boys. Some are from Lima, others from Callao, and the rest are from Huaral. We're all friends. Let's play a friendly game, and then we'll have a beer."

The soccer field was in an out-of-the-way clearing, but well suited for having a good time: good food, barbecue or fried chicken and meat, and plenty of cold drinks. In the distance, close to a coconut tree I saw Magnolia with a man who had on a colored shirt, hiding his face with dark sunglasses. Surely it was the Teacher. Close to him were three men watching his movements. The girl came up to say hi and talk a minute with my parents. She soon left.

Before the encounter I saw Isidro give some bills to my father who put them in his pocket.

The players looked at me kind of warily, and there was almost a fight when one of the Lima players got rough and stuck out his leg, making me fall. I did the same to him and there was almost a fight. Isidro just looked at them and calmed us down. He wasn't going to leave me. At the end of the game my father handed over a considerable amount of money to me, and said:

"Isidro is offering to buy the beer, but you have to make out like you're the one who's paying. That way they'll respect you. Oh, just in case, here they buy by the box, not by the beer. Don't make that mistake."

Isidro winked at me and raised a bottle of beer. My parents went home, leaving me in their company. Of course we ended up drunk, singing romantic ballads and finishing off with salsa dura. One of them asked every other minute if I had a camera to take photos of the "cooking." We went to a bar at the entrance to the town and kept drinking. I don't remember when Magnolia appeared and took me from the place to wake up in her bed, completely naked and with a pounding headache.

"Did we do anything?"

"Yes," answered the girl, "I'm your gift. He likes you." Magnolia was covered with a colored shirt, and wasn't wearing underwear. I could tell when she came close and kissed me. "You can stay until noon," she said, and lay back over the bed, with her mouth open.

That was all I could take. I had to make the most of the Teacher's present.

At eleven, three young men that said they were sent by Isidro arrived in a 4x4 to pick me up and bring me to the place where the product was being cooked. I brought my camera and we got in the vehicle.

My father gave me a hat to protect me from the intense heat.

After a half hour we arrived at a place where the road became narrow. We got out and continued on foot for maybe twenty minutes. We went over a small crest and from there you could see a good part of a valley filled with fruit trees. Before long we came to a placed filled with thorn bushes, protected by creepers and furious dogs who showed their teeth as soon as they saw us. Five people, looking nervous, pointed their weapons at us. Isido shouted from a distance:

"Don't be alarmed, boys, it's our guest. Come on, did you bring your camera? This is sensational. We're doing everything possible to follow the Teacher's orders. If we

I felt vulnerable. Why did they have to show me their movements? Did Isidro not know that I was a police officer? Maybe they brought me here to show me that they were capable of anything. I took a couple pictures and then sat on a log. Isidro brought me a bowl with masato, a fermented drink made from yuca.

"Enjoy, it's fresh." He looked around and ordered one of his men to be careful with the dogs. "Your father told me you're a police officer."

"Yeah," I affirmed, nodding.

"And not only that but that you work in narcotics."

"Why did you bring me here? Do you want to condemn me?"

"Relax, man. You're not here to fuck with us. That's what he told your father: if you don't fuck with us, we don't fuck with anyone. Your situation is kind of ironic. I know you're pretty damn scared, but don't worry. We're friends of your parents, and they treat us well. Till now you're behaving yourself. How long are you going to stay?"

"A week."

"That's enough. We're going to send a regular batch of merchandise these next couple days. If you want, you can come with us to bring it to the plane."

"Are you serious?" I asked, forgetting to drink the masato.

"What are you worried about, man? It's just a shipment."

"Thanks, but I barely have time to spend with my parents." Then I dared to ask, "You guys aren't afraid of the army?"

"We leave that for the Teacher. He's the one who takes

care of the details. Let's go, get up, keep taking photos so you can show them to the boss. Oh, just so you know, he doesn't know you're a police officer, and besides, you slept with Magnolia, his favorite girl."

The next day I thought that Magnolia would come to find me. So, I took out a chair and sat watching the road. My mother was a little nervous when she saw me because I kept rubbing my legs like I was cold.

"She's not going to come," she said, sitting by my side and offering me a mandarin. "Today it's her turn to visit the Teacher."

It angered me that the girl had gotten herself into this life. Couldn't she have stayed on her farm and taken care of her brothers?

I went outside to get some fresh air. The coca leaves were drying in the sun and my father, from time to time, would move them around with a broom made from fresh leaves. I got up and went to the kitchen to see what was cooking.

"Why don't we take a walk around the town?" asked my father when he saw I was a little worried. "We can go hang out at a bar till your mother finishes preparing lunch. I'd kill for a cold beer right now. Afterwards we'll bag up the leaves and carry them to the roof. But come on, son, maybe you'll see something that'll excite you."

A small truck picked us up when they saw us sweating on the side of the road and let us off at the entrance to town. I saw young soldiers posted close to the cement blocks that had been put at the entrance and exit of the town to control the population that marketed cocaine paste. It was just for appearances though, because with the intense heat, they let in ice cream, popsicles, or any other cold, wet thing that quenched their thirst, and they let any townsperson pass through that wanted to.

Far away, one could see a store that sold a variety of prod- [illegible] Magnolia's form walking towards the counter. I slowly turned my head and almost all the way in the back could see the Teacher with his hat in his hand and without his black sunglasses.

The two men who always accompanied him could be seen sitting at another table. The girl, noticing my presence, tried to hide her annoyance and covered the Teacher's line of sight. My father politely greeted the man, taking off his hat, and let him know that the farm was at his service. I think that that is what I heard. I asked for an ice-cold beer, and when I tried to get up to go to where Magnolia was, my father grabbed my shirt.

"What do you think you're doing?"

"I just want to say hi."

"She already saw you and doesn't want to talk. Let it be. Surely she'll come to the house later."

I drained my glass feeling something between bitterness and blindness. I asked for another bottle and my father said that was enough and besides, it was lunchtime. When we left, Isidro and some of his men were there in their 4x4.

"You want a ride home?" they asked as if our presence wasn't important. "We're picking up the merchandise. We'll probably send it out tomorrow. One thing, Artemio: when did you say you were going back to Lima?"

"Why?"

"It's a simple question, man. Don't let your nerves get away from you."

"Maybe in four days," I answered, and tried to pull my

father along to continue walking.

"It'd be better if you didn't put it off too much longer in this town," Isidro told me, pulling me by the arm. "You're a stranger here and it won't take long for them to notice what you do. We know your parents, but we don't know anything about their children, and frankly, we don't want to know. The arrival of an intruder makes us nervous. And you've been making us nervous ever since you arrived. Don't take it wrong; I'm just being sincere."

"But I spoke with you and with the partners about my son visiting," said my father, upset.

"Relax," smiled Isidro, "I'm just worried about the boy's safety. Let's go! Get in the car, we're heading that way anyway. This business pays well, but you have to watch it like gold. That's why we have to be protective. If something goes wrong, the blood flows and a lot of people end up floating in the river."

Magnolia arrived at six in the evening, and almost without giving me time, slapped a kiss on me. My mother turned her head and made a sign of disgust, which I understood. My father didn't care. She kept kissing me, hinting that we should go swimming in the stream at the end of the farm. "Don't take long," shouted my mother, reminding us that dinner was almost served.

The girl completely undressed and sat on a rock to watch me. Even though it was getting dark, I couldn't look away from the curves of her body; they began to make me crazy. She smiled when she saw how her nakedness made me nervous. I had seen her like this the other night, but now it seemed magical. I wasn't drunk and she didn't have any obligation. She submerged herself in the water and came up at my side, pulling me in. She offered temptation and I had no desire to resist. My hands clung to hers and I bit her neck and part of her ear. She gently moaned. When some birds got startled and flew off, we realized that we weren't alone. [illegible] I wanted to ask my father if he had gone to look for us, but I held back, so that when night came I couldn't sleep. Even though I held Magnolia in my arms, I thought I heard the sound of footsteps or murmuring behind the house, close to the stove.

The next day, after breakfast, we lay down on the hammock and filled each other with kisses, watching the coca leaves dry and throwing corncobs for the dogs to fetch. Close to noon the Teacher's men appeared with Isidro at the head, and the first thing they did was shoot at our dogs and insult me. Something had happened and they were looking for someone to blame.

"Fucking police!" he shouted with his mouth wide open, pointing his gun at my head. "You've brought us bad luck."

✶ ✶ ✶

Despite all the precautions they had taken, the army ambushed the Teacher's men just when they were sending out a half-ton of cocaine paste. They didn't have time to defend themselves. The result: one death and two detained, the plane was decommissioned, and the entire batch of the drug was sent away in a helicopter.

The Teacher was observing the maneuver from a distance and could do little to confront the army's surprise maneuver.

"This was the work of an informer," he said, beating one of his bodyguards with his fist. "Find the son of a bitch that snitched on us."

Isidro turned his head and remembered my name.

"It wasn't him," shouted Magnolia, coming up next to me.

The rage contained within Isidro let itself out through his heavy breathing. He beat the floor over and over. Then he went up to the woman and grabbed her.

"The Teacher needs to see you." His face contorted with rage when he came up to me. "And you, get in the truck. I need to vent on someone."

Two men pointed their weapons at me, obliging me to get in.

My father gave me advice:

"Don't open your mouth for any reason. If the Teacher manages to find out, you're a dead man."

The sun was starting to go down and a flash of lighting told me it was going to rain before night fell. Far away I could hear the roar of the Huallaga River and I felt a little scared.

✶✶✶

Standing in front of them, he realized he wouldn't have a second chance. It was too late to try to think of a way to buy more time. He raised his eyes to the tops of the trees that were gently swaying like a tropical hammock. He tried to remember, but his mind became cloudy: he was walking over a foam mattress that cushioned his fall, but at the same time it didn't let him defeat the heaviness that had taken possession of him. He opened his eyes, trying to remember what each person present looked like. He went from face to face, furrow to furrow, as if that would help alleviate his tension. But he realized that in each one of them he was dying a little more. Suddenly he paused: a face. Magnolia! The everlasting Magnolia, the girl he made love with anywhere he could. She didn't cry because that was how she was: serene before any difficult situation, she never lost hope. But now that he was in front of

weapons cocked, she must have seriously been thinking about crying.

Silence. A cold stab of pain made his body tremble, rising from his feet to rest at his teeth and make him chatter. Then there was an order and the rest was a maze of white clouds that circled around his eyes. And then he managed to make out thick tears falling from Magnolia's eyes.

****

Night fell in Tocache. The Huallaga River trembles when it rains and lets go of sticks and logs that get washed up on the islands or wedged in the wide ports. And sometimes it uncovers deformed bodies eaten by fish, floating to an unknown destination, getting lost in the whirlpools, destroyed, until sinking in the eddies of a rough section of rapids. The rain said goodbye to Magnolia, who at the bottom of the river was wearing the dress that the Teacher had given her. She left ready for the party, with nothing to hold her back, hardly the fish that hide in her armpits, among her empty eye sockets, in her hair, and between her teeth, leaving through her mouth to jump out of the water as if calling the mermaids who will come to bring her to the bottom of the Huallaga.

JOHN CLARK

I DON'T KNOW why they gave him that name. But it fit him well despite the fact that they didn't make fun of his last name: Shupingahua. This was his mother's fault, who wasn't able to hold onto his father, a traveler who had slept with her after going to the patron saint celebrations in Quinilla for the Saint Rose festivities. He left before the roosters could announce the coming of the day. Obdulia barely had time to see how he wore his hat. He left through the back part of the house, trying not to make noise, so that her brothers and her father wouldn't follow him with the dogs, like she had threatened, if he stepped outside. Before the boy disappeared, she had asked him his name.

"John," he answered, almost whispering. She believed him. And she couldn't hear his last name.

When he was born, his mother didn't know what name to give him until her older brother showed her a magazine where a reporter, in a magic moment, wore a blue uniform and flew through the skies, trying to stop crime. This reporter's name was Clark Kent. She liked Clark, so she associated it with John.

Two years later Obdulia joined Nixon Shupingahua Fasanando, who had a five-year-old son, and he treated her son as his own. John Clark Shupingahua didn't have anything in common with Nixon. There were marked differences that jumped out when one looked at them.

When he started getting older, John would go out in search of adventure. He was in Iquitos for a long time. Then he went to Pucallpa, close to the port, in the company of [illegible] causing problems, disappearing into the Hoyada neighborhood. He got used to the easy life, and as if it was the most natural thing, he began going to the bars and brothels, waking up in bed with prostitutes, smelling like cheap tobacco.

When they asked his name he would only say people called him John Clark. Many of them believed it because his athletic build, blue eyes, curly hair, and white face dispelled any doubt. They were even jealous of his ostentatious last name. A friend asked if he wanted to come to Lima with him for a while and that was how he settled in the Mirones Bajo neighborhood. There, in the company of "Santana" and "Bujurqui," they would wait in the night, close to a place called El Montón, to assault people passing through and acquire some money. John Clark was getting used to this easy life, until one night a group of boys stood up to them and gave them a thrashing, leaving them lying in puddles of blood. Then his life turned around, and before he could think twice, he was working in a ceramics factory. There he shined. His athletic form and features played an important role. He legally changed his last name to Smith, so that his complete name was John Clark Smith. The Pole in charge of his area didn't believe him, but didn't care as long as he worked and didn't cause any problems.

He fell in love with Ivón Salcedo, with whom he went out with for more than a year. He only broke up with her when she told him she was pregnant. He quit his job, sold all his things, and with the money went to Tingo María. There he found out that Ivón had given birth to a baby boy.

He shrugged his shoulders and without the least remorse, asked his brother what he could invest his money in. His brother advised him that in Tocache he could buy "coke" and send it with the "mules."

"Are you being serious?" he asked, without losing his surprise.

He had known that his brother had been mixed up for many years in a business that let him live comfortably. And he was never able to ask him anything about it, maybe because he did it discreetly. But Uchiza and Tocache were becoming infamous for shady business. He suddenly felt worried, scared, and a shiver even began to run up his spine.

"Of course, man," answered his brother, who was getting some air in the rocking chair. "Look for Russo Chujutalli or Isidro Tuanama. They're my friends and will help set you up. Oh, and get rid of Smith for your last name, it sounds like isma, or shit, the way you have it. Keep Shupingahua, it's the last name my father gave you."

With his new friends he only made three deliveries. They acquired the "mules" for him that travelled towards Pucallpa and Iquitos, until an old woman, 70 years old, was caught in Tingo María with the merchandise concealed next to her stomach. She didn't say anything and the police weren't strict in the interrogation either. They knew that one of the owners of the cocaine would present themselves to fix the problem. They did it through a lawyer well known by the police. The old woman was freed but the merchandise wasn't. John Clark lost everything. Then, with his new friends, they came up with the idea of assaulting travelers on the highway who they suspected might be coming to buy cocaine in Tocache. They did this for a month, until Isidro told him he should give it a rest because John's features were easy to identify. With the little that he had collected, he found a place to stay in ... ... the opportunity to present itself.

They told him that all the buyers and sellers frequently went to The Junction, but that there also might be partners or undercover military there. It was risky, but he had to take his chances. There he met Douglas, and with him everything changed, because from that moment everything was planned and Douglas, a teacher fallen on hard times, knew how to organize and give orders. Little by little he was imposing his authority until he was respected and became known as the Teacher.

He was the one who had the job of sending out the shipment of a half-ton of cocaine paste from the small airport in Tocache.

"If everything goes well," said the Teacher, "we'll have more orders. We're working with people from Colombia. They have eyes and ears everywhere. If something goes wrong, we'll be floating down the Huallaga River."

That night he went to Magnolia and after having some drinks made a comment to her about the operation. Now he regrets that he didn't notice. When the army fell on top of them, John knew that the Teacher would be looking for a snitch. Maybe he would suspect him or Magnolia.

"What's your name?" asked the soldier, grabbing him by the neck.

"John Clark Smith," he answered, raising his head.

He heard the soldiers laugh. "A Smith in Tocache? Are you fucking serious?"

"Come on, tell us the truth," they replied angrily. "We know everything about you."

Some tears fell from John's eyes and he thought of Ivón Salcedo and the son that he would never know. There was a military helicopter waiting to transport the "goods" and the people who had been detained. He knew that they wouldn't arrive at their destination. He became desperate, and the woods that were close seemed like a good refuge to take shelter in. He just had to push away the young soldier and begin running. It would also only be a couple of seconds before he felt the bullets riddling his body.

LEYDITH

RUN WAS the first thing that occurred to her. She didn't have time to pack her things, barely a small suitcase that she tied tightly. She put on her old tennis shoes covered in mud and left through the back so she could go towards the river. They wouldn't waste time. "Someone talked," Leonor had told her. "I don't know why Isidro is looking for you, but it smells bad to me."

Her feet got tangled in the lianas and roots that hindered her movement towards the river. She had to get to the shore and follow it downriver. She was exhausted and filled with fear. Her countenance became contorted and her body froze when she heard footsteps in the reeds. She picked up a stick and got ready to defend herself, but it was just a dog coming out to meet her. She heard voices and barely had time to hide in the undergrowth. When they left, she figured that it must be around three in the afternoon, left her hiding place, and went out on the riverbank. It would take between fifteen and twenty minutes to get to the Tocache exit and wait for a bus or pickup to appear that was heading somewhere, anywhere, as long as it was far from this place. She went up the small hill that separated the port from the town and saw some men getting out of a 4x4. She noticed that they were armed, and thought she recognized Isidro. How did he escape the ambush that the Teacher and his men had fallen prey to?

She realized she had urinated on herself, but she didn't care. She was really scared and knew that they were capable of anything. Leydith remembered her mother and her child, [illegible] use as a weapon just in case they found her.

Leydith was determined to escape at all costs. If they didn't find her, she would arrive in Progreso, and from there could go to Tingo María: they wouldn't follow her there, though she was sure that they wouldn't leave her in peace after what Leonor mentioned had happened to the Teacher's men. If she went the other direction and was lucky, she would get to Madre Mía, where there was a military base, but she didn't want to risk it. She could try throwing herself into the river and swim downstream, but she'd never get around the obstacles of Cayumba and Sábalo Yacu. She began to cry, covering her face. It would be night soon. She didn't even think about going out to the road unless a bus drove by. Nor would she look for help if she wasn't sure they were good people. There was only one highway and it would be controlled. But it was her only salvation. How long could she resist?

✳ ✳ ✳

Leydith was fifteen when she got pregnant thanks to Fausto, her father's friend that used to visit on Saturday afternoons and drink a beer. She liked Fausto, and being alone with him was like a gift. Nevertheless, what happened afterwards would weigh down on her and oblige her to make a decision that would hurt her parents. The boy didn't want anything to do with the baby, and she ran away one night from Moyobamba and travelled far, to Juanjui, in the middle of spring. There she met Kely and Andico, friends who helped her find a place to stay in the house of a friend who was serving a jail sentence in Tarapoto. Kely fell in love with Leydith even though she was pregnant, but she told him that she wasn't looking for love. She wanted to work, and found a job in a bar with Aleja, a woman who was getting older and was looking for fifteen-year-old girls to serve her clients.

When her son was born, Kely had no problem continuing to help her. They fell in love and he asked the owner of the bar if she could stay there. Aleja gave her a filthy narrow place to sleep, hardly a room, where Kely would visit her. One morning her mother appeared and told her to come back to Moyobamba. She refused, and the woman took her newborn son. The owner of the bar told her to look for somewhere else to stay because she didn't want any problems. Leydith left Juanjui and headed to Tocache to look for work. Kely went with her. For a while they were coca leaf harvesters, in Bajo Limón, putting up with the hot sun on their backs.

One Saturday afternoon, while they having cold drinks at The Junction, some soldiers appeared, and amid gunshots and shouting, they began to carry off all the young men that were there. The lovers hid out back and left through the garden. But they didn't get far before a bullet hit Kely's leg. Leydith tried to help him, but he told her to keep running and look for refuge where she could because he knew that soldiers don't ask questions.

Kely didn't appear that night or ever again. Leydith stayed out of sight for a while and then, when she was sure she wouldn't be followed, went to town to look for work in the bars. There she became a prostitute. Her idea was to save money and then return to Moyobamba. She met Magnolia, who would become the Teacher's lover, and a police officer that was on vacation. She traveled to Sión with Magnolia, to obtain a gift for the boss' close friends. And it was Magnolia who told her about the shipment of a half-ton of cocaine paste that they were preparing. And when Leonor told her about Isidro's weird visit, she grabbed what she could and left through the back door of the house. She just wanted to escape because she too had let a comment slip about the shipment to a friend she laid from time to time, and whose name she couldn't remember. And if the men who murdered the Teacher found out, she'd be one more body floating down the Huallaga River.

* * *

From her hiding place she could make out a military patrol that was coming to control the exit and arrival of buses and pickups. Isidro spoke with them and offered them cigarettes while his hands pointed towards the woods and river. Then they burst out laughing. Leydith snuck closer, crouching low, trying to hear what they were saying. She knew she was taking a risk. Then, in the back of a pickup she made out Leonor's figure. My God! Why didn't he ask for help from the soldiers? She didn't want to think any more. Some dogs started barking. She stood there for a couple seconds, trembling, without really wanting to even move. Before she began to run, she saw that Isidro had raised his head towards her hiding place and was pointing with his fingers. Leydith began to groan and thought of Kely and his indifferent face when he had pleaded for her to leave so the soldiers wouldn't take her away.

The sound of barking dogs was getting closer. This time she knew they were coming up behind her. Isidro had gone for help and didn't care that the soldiers were there. She shook her head several times. Slapping herself, she slid down to the bank of the river, walking over the rocks and grabbing the roots of the trees that hung down into the water. She heard voices. Leydith began to cry when she tripped on a liana. Then she thought of her son and what he would be doing now. Surely her mother would be walking him through the yard, showing him the nests of the hens or grabbing limes to make mechado. She dried her tears and walked into the water. But she ran into a little problem: the small bank she was following got too steep and dropped down a ravine into deep water below.

Without caring she jumped down the slope into the water of the river and swam back out so that the dogs wouldn't smell her scent. She hid in a tree that had a root going all the way to the shore of the river. When she no longer heard anything, she climbed down and looked towards the road. Nothing. It was empty. The silence penetrated her soul and took possession of her body. She began to shiver. She was cold and the night was on top of her. She walked into the forest without daring to come out. She got to a rocky place, having no idea how long it took her to get there. Leydith stopped close to a tall bank where she could hear the murmuring of the river and the beating of the small waves over the rocks below. She thought of the bad stretches of the river that devoured boats and canoes. Tiredness took over and she fell asleep with her wet clothing stuck to her body. She dreamed about Leonor warning her of Isidro's presence. Then her son arrived, holding her mother's hand, with Kely behind them, signaling her to run after them. She stayed to gaze at her son but he kept insisting. Then she heard a growl that made her mother run while Kely slowly faded away.

[illegible] up [illegible] in [illegible] The jungle was completely silent. The night put everything to sleep even though she thought she heard murmuring coming from the thicket. She narrowed her sight and thought she could make out two lanterns. "Fireflies," she thought. Too late.

"So you were the snitch," said a voice she couldn't see.

Leydith jumped, stood up, and took a couple steps in retreat. The ravine was close to her. She didn't say anything. She was scared and feared for her life. Three men advanced, speaking to her, threatening her. One of them had a machete in his hands.

"Sorry, you're just a whore that made a mistake. We rape snitches and cut out their tongues so that their mouth never runs off again."

She didn't plead with them or even really think of it as a possibility. She was fed up with living a life that was going from bad to worse.

"Don't you want to know what happened to Leonor?" one of the men asked.

She was close to the ravine and, backing up, her feet had just enough space to throw herself into the depths of the river. It must have been close to four in the morning and the jungle was filled with animals running and fluttering when the shots were heard.

While she fell, her eyes closed and she dreamed that she defeated Cayumba and Sábalo Yacu, and that she swam among the froth in the bad stretches of the river, and that the virgin that was hidden among the cracks of the narrow channel smiled at her and looked at her with eyes filled with tenderness. It reminded her of her son that was appearing little by little, opening his arms, waiting for her in her hometown, past the bridge where one time she had thought to buy a piece of land and plant orchids.